The lion, the lord, the
and the Belt and Road
Robin Thomas

abuddhapress@yahoo.com

ISBN: 9798867474997

Robin Thomas 2023-24

®™©

Alien Buddha Press 2023-24

The following is a work of fiction. Any similarities to actual people, places, or events, unless deliberately expressed otherwise by the author are purely coincidental.

In which Snidge is enjoined to look sharp

'Well,' said Lord Merrychip, 'that's me for poetry. Damned if I know where the next one's comin' from.' He beat a retreat to his shed, lit his pipe and leant back in his dilapidated but soft and comfortable leather chair. Amid clouds of noxious smoke he wondered about the great French master of deconstruction, about Aristotle, his favourite but perhaps superannuated hunter and about dinner – would there be one or two pork chops today? His reveries were interrupted by the arrival of Snidge, gardener-in-chief, personal batman, student of Galen. 'Mornin' sir,' said he, his hand rising to a clumsy salute, 'got yer new Derrida 'ere sir, suggest yer start at p.103, up to there is bit ploddin'. Oh I beg your pardon, your lordship, that was my gardening voice.' 'No matter, thankee Snidge,' replied Lord M, 'I'll follow your suggestion, now get on and clean me boots, I fancy a gallop after me pipe – think I'll pop in and see Featherstonehaugh, find out if he's got that new consignment of Siberian tea. And the old bugger's writin'

Zen and the Russian battle tank, in Onegin stanzas, I think, and I want to see how he's gettin' on. Like you to have a look too, Snidge, when yer've finished those boots, look sharp now!' The great lord paused to draw on his pipe, 'Oh and translate me a couple of passages from The Decameron if you please, Snidge.'

'What have we got here?'

The great lord had been more than satisfied with the discussion on the Pushkin/Zen project – Featherstonehaugh was now focussing on the second generation T34 tank and Middle Chinese Zen and had argued forcefully that this was a better fit with Pushkin's stanza form – but was disappointed with the non-appearance of permafrost tea which he had been particularly looking forward to. He left Featherstonehaugh House on Aristotle and trotted thoughtfully up the road. As he rode he considered Featherstonehaugh's sideways shift for a moment: 'Yes, better fit altogether.' before moving on to a subject closer to his heart: he muttered something to himself about Swedish tea ceremonies, allowing himself a half-smile. 'Let that Frenchy deconstruct that!' he said to himself and chuckled. 'Out of my way, you scoundrel.' he shouted at a passing swineherd, cleared the fence and began to gallop towards a gap in the trees. 'Blessed fella Dante.' said he, 'couldn't see a stand of trees without conjurin' up a whole underworld, and a damned unpleasant one at that.'

Heideggar

As if in answer to his lordship's ruminations on the author of the Comedia there came a gurgle from the nearby brook, causing Aristotle to mince his forelocks a little and shake his mane. Lord M, noticing this small sideways stagger, superb horseman that he was, reached for his riding whip, then desisted, as if caught on the horns of an argument between Heideggar and Rousseau on the true nature of the authentic. 'Social or individual life.' he wondered before standing on the stirrups and again forging ahead. 'Wooah,' he shouted to his Athenian stallion, 'we have some visitors I see.' Aristotle came smoothly to a halt, careful not to spatter the couple below in the lane.

Fustian

'Oh most sorry to be in your way,/ your lordship,' said a bedraggled looking lad, clothed roughly in fustian and pushing a sweet-looking but equally roughly dressed girl behind him as if to protect her, 'we was only sticking labels to/ the trees, so people can identify/ their names, sir.' 'It is not for common folk to be educators,' thundered Lord M, 'take them down at once!'

In which the small birds chatter

Having delivered this admonishment Lord M touched gently the sides of his heroic steed with his spurs, kept purposely blunt so as not to damage him and, rising and falling in the saddle, cantered him on down the lane. The bushes on both sides seemed to be singing, so many were the birds. The great lord would have felt happy to be alive were his brain not overburdened with a knotty problem: *was Popper a Positivist? Carnap thought so.* The question seemed at odds with the sunny day, the sparkling, rustling leaves, the platoons, nay the divisions of small birds chattering their own stories, their own questions, debating their own existential status. 'Must ask Snidge,' said his lordship to himself, 'Sandhurst was hopeless, all sorts of stuff about caltraps, ravelins, outerworks, bastions, madder, polearms, but nothin' on anythin' of any use to anyone.'

'I don't think so'

The two commoners, Pontius Pilates and Milkmaid Mary-Anne stood looking after him, their ragged clothes flapping forlornly. 'True is it that we tend to talk in free/ verse' said Pontius to his Mary-Anne. 'No,' said she, 'I don't think so.' 'I'm not so sure my sweet,' said he to her/ 'let's go and take the labels down right now,' he said, and off they went to collect them. 'What shall we do now that they have no names? /Mary I look for your advice.' 'I see you dropped the 'Anne' for the sake of the scansion,' said she, 'let them name themselves.'

'Lacking words to describe it'

Continuing his journey along the lane, Lord M came upon something he had not seen before – a kind of small electric windmill, though he lacked words so to describe it, being semi-illiterate, except in the realms of philosophy and abstract literary theory. He also didn't know how electric windmills worked – small, medium *or* large – having been educated only in dead languages and military architecture. 'Whooah, Stagirite,' (he was in that kind of mood), 'let's take a look-see old fella.' So they stopped and he dismounted, unnecessarily tying the loyal horse to a nearby thorn tree. On closer inspection the purpose of the machine was revealed – it was for chopping logic.

'One day …'

The young people left the trees to name themselves. Whether they did so we shall never know. 'Let's smooth them out and take them home with us.'/ said Pontius. 'OK,' said Mary-Anne, 'paper's so expensive we can't afford to waste any. My dad could do with something to turn them from a crumpled mess into proper paper suitable for scribbling on – but probably nothing's been invented yet to do that. One day he'll learn to read and write, then I suppose he'll compose that Magnum Opus he keeps promising us.'

Occam

Lord M had never seen one of these before, certainly not an electric one. He could see though what you had to do – you'd to open the hatch at the top, throw in as much logic as you could get into the space, and press that little button over there labelled 'Occam's Razor'. Then it would rumble into action, spitting invalid arguments and meaningless propositions into that container at the side (there was room for two containers so that Schrodinger's cat, if it got too close, could find itself in two containers at once, providing two had been supplied. If there were only one, the cat would be in one container at once). Lord M could see what to do but couldn't bring himself to perform an act properly in the sphere of a common person. 'I wish Snidge were here!' he murmured. 'If only I knew how to use my mobile to make telephone calls I could get him over here haste post haste dispatch.'

In which Jenny leaves the building

The machine, No.17, had been invented by Jenny Rennes, who now looked up from her cup of tea at the incoming messages telling her that it was being interfered with. Stopping only to reach for the manual – Wittgenstein's Tractatus Logico-Philosphicus (she found the first edition most suitable) – and her boots, she left the Inventors' Institute and set out towards the machine on her penny-farthing, wobbling across the ploughed fields and along the rutted lanes towards her object until there was a bump.

In which they trudge homewards

'Where is an inventor when you need one?' said Mary-Anne crossly. 'We shall not find one such as that.' said Pon/tious as he looked with sadness at his friend. Homewards trudged they their weary way, stopping only to wash their faces in the sparkling brook that gurgled and fizzed beside them. They came to the familiar cross-lane and turned into it, greeted first by a shining eyed cow, Bets-y-Coed, then Percy the shire horse and finally by pet lion, Ralph, but they were too morose to notice.

Dogmatic slumber (1)

As if summoned by the trill of a mobile phone, arrived Snidge on his scooter. 'Reporting for duty.' your lordship, said he. 'Ah yes, Snidge, good fella, see that button there, no, that one, press it if you please.' 'I wouldn't do that if I were you sir.' 'Why not, Snidge, and I'm not proposing to do it myself, that's why I would have summoned you.' 'I understand, your lordship, but what I meant is that it may not be advisable to push that button, sir.' 'Why on earth not, Snidge?' 'Not quite sure, sir, but I have a bad feeling about it.' 'Bad feelin', poppycock, what'cha doing with feelin's anyway? I know you're a superior kind of common person, but I don't see the logic of someone in your situation having to do with feelin's.' (although Snidge had the rank of only a senior common person, so to speak, Lord M had a surprising amount of respect for him. Mind you he wouldn't wish to exaggerate or indeed even acknowledge this). 'While we think about it, read me a couple of paras from one of those Critiques, in

German.' Snidge was not best pleased, he'd had an unfortunate experience with buttons but nothing can be said about that here as it may be covered by an injunction.

In which Jenny stops to think

Jenny quickly invented a pump suitable for a solid tyre and was back on the farthing, racing towards her object. She came out into the main lane but suddenly noticed a low bridge marked LOW BRIDGE. She leapt off her machine and slid it sideways under the arch, crouching as she did so and successfully reached the other side only to find another sign INVENTORS FORBIDDEN. 'Typical of the countryside!' she said to herself and turned sadly back. 'I've done enough sliding sideways and crouching for one day' she said to herself and stopped to think. 'A cup of tea would be nice, but where to get one in the middle of the countryside?'

Pastries

'Was that a lion I saw in the lane?'/ said Ponty, looking quite perturbéd. 'I'm afraid it was,' said Mary-Anne, 'he's there because of a category mistake.' 'Well never mind that now, for sure/ it must be time for our delicious tea.' Mary-Anne's mum was famous in those parts for her blackwater rose tea and medieval Danish pastries and they were both looking forward to them, even if they were members of the lower orders with correspondingly rough and ready taste buds (aristocrats have around 10,000 of them, whereas commoners may have as few as nine). And so they proceeded to Mary-Anne's mum's hovel.

'Something a bit different'

Then Jenny had a bit of a brainwave: 'I'm an inventor. What would an inventor do in this situation?' She looked and looked, then thought and thought and started to work on the farthing – a bit off here, move this there, lengthen this a bit, and in no time at all there, shining, new and ready to go was a Tuppence Ha'penny. 'Oh what a nuisance, I still can't get under the tunnel. It still won't allow inventors. What I need is something a bit different, something that seems like it's going this way but in fact goes that way. There, that should do the trick. I'll call it a boris.'

'A resourceful chap'

Lord M had been delivered into a rhapsody by Snidge's reading, even though the pronunciation of the latter was somewhat modern and he had forgotten all about trying to start the strange machine. 'Another twenty-three and a bit volumes.' his lordship breathed in an ecstasy of unmitigated pleasure. 'Righto, Snidge,' says he, 'I'd like a cup of tea and a piece of medieval cake please.' 'Thank you for your kind instructions, sir, but, ahem, I'm not sure where we are to find tea and cake in this corner of the shire.' 'You're a resourceful chap, for, or perhaps because you are, a commoner, Snidge, go and find some, if you please.' 'What I need is an electric tea and cake maker and a supply of electricity.' Snidge murmured to himself.

Quebec

Mary-Anne's mum had been a lion tamer in a small way and part time attorney at law (she had practised in Quebec where the word 'attorney' is used only as the English term for 'avocat', that is when she could find the time – being a lion tamer is exceptionally intense and of course they don't have lions in Quebec. If they did they'd be called 'leons', also true in the Philippines). 'Is that the reason why there is a lion/ in the lane that we have come along' asked Pontius. 'Of course not, I told you how that happened.' said Mary-Anne, now becoming a little irritated. They knocked where the door would have been and entered. 'ello, my leetle ones, assiettez-vous, s'il vous plait.' Mary-Anne's mum was, despite her lowly place in life, a bit posh. That's why she spoke in Franglais.

Inveigling

Using the newly invented boris, Jenny inveigled her way under the bridge and rode along the road thus made legally accessible. She was now re-assaulted by the idea of tea. She started looking around for some but eventually the sensible thought came to her 'I'm an inventor, not a discoverer.' This latter distinction perhaps at least partially explained why she passed by a tea shoppe while having such sensible thoughts. 'What materials do I need.' she said out loud to herself, in case she wasn't listening, 'I need some clay to fashion a pot, some twigs to set light to, something nice and hot, a kilt or something like that, to fire the pot. I need to boil the water – the water! Yes, I need water – grass for drying into tea bags, some slippery elm bark powder for seasoning and papyrus for the cups.' All these were readily available of course and she set to work. Then she really had to get on and find No.17.

Picture Theory

Mary-Anne's mum was happiest when she was preparing tea. Being of superior intelligence she naturally made use of Wittgenstein's picture theory to convert her (and only her) thought of tea into the reality of that hot brown watery substance that everyone without exception loves to distraction, unless they prefer coffee. And she liked to make use of Duns Scotus in her development of medieval pastries. She did not need to go to Denmark to make superior baked goods, even if they did have a smart new bridge connecting them to Sweden. And her favourite room in the hovel was the tea ceremony room, built by Mary-Anne's dad before he left for China with Featherstonehaugh's brother. There the three of them sat, contentedly eating and drinking, one wistfully thinking of her husband.

Snidge's quest

The resourceful Snidge went about looking for tea. He was no fool. He would not expect to find tea and cake under hedgerows or in chuckling brooks, and thought narrow rural lanes were equally unlikely to provide for his master's needs. He decided that the best thing to do was sniff, so that's what he did. Sure enough, he smelt electricity, 'That's electricity,' he said to himself and to anyone else who was listening, 'and where there's electricity you can't be far from a kettle, and where there's a kettle … .' He was wrong of course, a rare but not inconceivably unlikely occurrence. So he continued his search, sniffing, to which he added looking and indeed listening, just in case.

The Turing Machine

While Jenny was inventing how to make tea under inauspicious circumstances and outlining the paper she would write on the subject, her head was buzzing with all kinds of ideas, and as is often the case with inventors, and every now and then a handy one popped up. She was a very modern young person, mightily influenced by modern thinkers. She was particularly impressed by Dirac's updating of Einstein and thought that she might have a go at updating Dirac himself when she had a spare afternoon. One of the ideas she had while pondering Einstein and Dirac was that she could probably convert the logic chopper, providing there was enough logic to chop and so provide the necessary power, into a space-time machine (of course the tides of time would have to be right if it were to work properly). There was a small but not insignificant further advantage in this plan – a space-time machine was pretty much bound to have the facility to convert wastepaper into pristine white writing paper. This might be of some use to someone. She'd have to return to the laboratory and do some updates on her model of the Turing machine, run it a couple of times and test it out, but that could wait, although she did foresee problems with the woman/machine interface if she didn't do the updates. In the meantime, while she was inventing how to make tea, she could think out the basic steps from electric windmill to full-fledged space-time machine, hoping not to mix up the two thought processes.

Deptford and an existential displacement

Mary-Anne's dad had gone to China as personal servant to Featherstonehaugh's brother but they had somehow become separated and he subsequently discovered himself to have been thrown into the role of a labourer on the Hong Kong–Shanghai railway. The work had been arduous with only the occasional meal of gritty rice or slithery noodles to keep him and his workmates alive. There were so many of them that they had to sleep standing up, no wonder they got tired. What really kept him going though was Confucius, a copy of whose works he had picked up in an opium den in Deptford. He was inspired by this to learn Cantonese. What he didn't quite realise was that the copy he had needed to be read in Mandarin: a phrase like 'nong pha nu ping dra on' may mean 'I sing to your everlasting form' in Cantonese but 'concrete sets too quickly if you're not careful and can trap a golden dragon's feet, rendering it immobile' in Mandarin. Confusion is always possible if language is misused as

Mary-Anne's dad found out on more than one occasion. He had several times had to quote Confucius to himself: 'When anger rises think of the consequences.' ('hong wo con ping so' in Cantonese, 'he na woo rong ning' in Mandarin).

Featherstonehaugh's brother

had gone to China in support of his brother's researches and expected particularly to be able to follow up Middle Chinese Zen there. He didn't realise at first that he was in entirely the wrong part of what everybody knows is a very large country and there were all kinds of complicated permissions to be obtained before he could travel anywhere, and of course he didn't have Mary-Anne's dad to assist him. If only the Shanghai to Hong Kong railway were finished! Anyway as soon as he had obtained the appropriate and correctly stamped documents he set off in a caravan (no reference to *Caravan* by Juan Tizol, once a trombonist with Duke Ellington, is intended here) pulled by camels. He chose this method of locomotion because it aligned with his political views: he was embarrassed by his status as an aristocrat (People with names like Featherstonehaugh are always aristocrats) and the fact that he had landed on a pile of money when he'd been tossed into the world. Nevertheless the caravan was very comfortable and stopped every now and then so that he could be plied with regional cooking at a caravanserai, which was mostly very good, although he wasn't that keen on the spiders. It was while he was sipping a well earnt Moutai brandy in the fourth month of the journey that Featherstonehaugh's brother noticed a cupboard in the luxurious caravan labelled 'Zen – complete works about.' There, much to his amazement, he found exactly what he needed. He immediately sent an email to his brother with the necessary documents attached and made ready to change direction towards Siberia, in furtherance of his and his brother's aims. 'Perhaps I'll go by tram.' he said to himself.

Porsches in unfortunate colours

Looking's probably best if you're looking for tea, so this is what Snidge mostly did. And while he did so he rehearsed his reasons for refuting Kant, especially the vexed notion of knowledge that was a priori and yet synthetic, and how he was to convince his lordship without upsetting him for he (the latter) was a sensitive soul and a great Kantian. While in this state of mind, Snidge did not notice the tea shoppe passing by to his left as he trudged along a kind of major lane with a bridge in the distance. 'A bridge.' he thought to himself, 'Could that be the great bridge festooned with autistic women driving yellowish-brown Porsches linking Malmo and Copenhagen and inhabiting Scandinavian crime dramas? Or might it be the bridge between relativity and quantum mechanics so long sought after by physicists, or indeed that between linguistic and non-linguistic reality Wittgenstein puzzled over for decades?'

The Great Tradition

Lord M was not used to being by himself, he could hardly put his own shoes on, although he was adept at leaping on to his horse providing Snidge was there to hold its reins and whisper into its ear, to provide a helpful shove and remove the step ladder. He did not expect to send for tea and not find it hurtling into his presence the next minute. He was rather put out by the lack of bell pulls for summoning the servant class. 'Who on earth designed this countryside business.' he said to himself, rather chagrined. To calm himself down he went through the reasons Kingie Leavis had for including Lawrence in *The Great Tradition.* 'Funny little buggar.' he muttered.

Chuckles

'Buggar,' she said to herself, 'I think I *have* mixed them up,' contemplating a giant shiny brown teapot, standing there like a strangely shaped stele, like a monument to the history of tea-making or to the mixings up of thought processes. The irony of a giant teapot which clearly could not deliver the ardently-desired brown liquid struck her forcibly and she chuckled softly in an inventor's way. 'But I wonder if it has space-time capabilities? Well there's only one way to find out.' What she needed was a giant teaspoon and none was to be found, search though she might. 'If I could find No.17, I might be able to use that. In the meantime, I need some tea. At least I've invented how to make some!'

Quizzics

'You did say I believe it was a cat/egory mistake,' said Pontius, sipping his tea, 'and do you think that makes him speak/ in tongues not natural to a lion?', Mary-Anne looking quizzically the while. 'More tea?' said Mary-Anne's mum, 'You can see for yourself – Ralph's coming round later for some marmalade cake and to get a thorn taken out of his paw.' Sure enough, about an hour later, just as Pontius was reaching for his third (and last – there weren't any more) non-Scandinavian pastry, Ralph turned up. 'Moo.' he said politely.

Belgium

Snidge passed a young woman dressed in a kind of Victorian lab-coat who seemed lost in thought or at least in contemplation and wondered if he should stop to help. 'Well no,' he said to himself, 'it would be intruding on her thoughts I think, and in any case, I've work to do.' 'Now what was it I had to do?' he said to himself. He saw the lane-side tea shoppe again but hurried past. 'I could do with a cup of tea, but I just haven't time ... now what was it I had to do?' (he had a habit of repeating himself when perplexed). He was of course also lost in metaphysical thought and wondered if, one day, perhaps in retirement, if his lordship would ever let him retire, he would be able to embark upon that great, self-imposed task – the study of racehorse, football team and early twentieth-century dreadnought names in relation to the development of scholastic philosophy between 1171 and 1173 in the lower of the Low Countries.

Musing (1)

Lord M wondered idly where Snidge had got to. 'Does he in fact exist,' he mused, 'now he's out of my sight.' He found a sofa in a convenient hedgerow and sat down. He found it much easier to muse sitting down but didn't always have much to muse about, or to put it slightly differently, he found musing rather more satisfactory if Snidge were there with a tray of tea things and toast, cake or brandy, depending on the time of day and waiting to offer his advice, should it be called for, which it usually was. And where was Aristotle? 'Ah, I remember, he's tied to a thorn tree.' The trouble with thorn trees is that they are prickly but not very visible, being rather thin. Lord M looked around for a thorn tree. Not being so good at thorn tree recognition, he was used to identifying them by their being tied to a horse. He couldn't see a horse, so couldn't identify a tree, so couldn't find his horse.

Musing (2)

Mary-Anne's dad, let's call him Frank, and to be fair his name *was* Frank, was coming to the end of his service on the railway line and wondered to himself what he ought to do next. 'I wonder if there's a vacancy for a Confucius scholar around here,' he said to himself, 'and if so, how I'd find out.' He paused deep in thought for a moment, a sackful of permanent way ballast in his hand, until the foreman, not unreasonably, said to him, 'I am mindful of a lack of progress on your section of the line and hope you are too. If it pleases you would you mind speeding up a teeny bit?' 'I'm terribly sorry, sir, but I was musing.' 'Oh, that's alright then, if I'd known you were musing I wouldn't have spoken to you in that rough way. I request that you continue laying the track when you have completed your current musings.'

No.17

'Now where exactly *was* No.17?' Jenny frowned to herself in that gentle way of hers. 'I'm sure it was over here, but it could be over there I suppose.' Jenny climbed onto a nearby teapot to get a better view. 'Can't see it anywhere, oh wait a minute there it is on the other side of that bridge.' Jenny made her way towards it on her tuppence. She kept mainly to the complex system of interlaced and intercrossing country lanes to avoid going over the rutted fields which tuppences are not good at and found her way to it not without frequent reference to her prized Tractatus.

42

'Despite his hulking size and fierce appearance ...'

So Ralph returned up the farm lane to his field. Despite his hulking size and fierce appearance, no one was frightened of him, neither the cows nor the sheep nor the mice and voles, the little birds, not even the beetles, ants and wildflowers were afraid. For Ralph was a gentle creature, especially since he'd become a vegetarian. No doubt some of this was due to the category error that had installed a lion which should have been in Africa where of course he would have been extremely fierce, to a field in the English countryside. Anyway, Ralph who would have had plenty to do in Africa just being fierce, was at a bit of a loss as to what to do with the rest of his day. There wasn't much point in just being gentle.

In which Snidge finds himself in strange territory

The truth is that Snidge had completely forgotten what it was he was looking for, or even if he was looking for anything. He'd got involved in some very strange territory – 'Why is there not an anything?' he asked the universe. This is the kind of question that can get you going along quite strange pathways, not to mention trees up which if you are not careful you will find yourself barking. 'I'm thirsty.' was his next thought. 'Tea.' was the subsequent one and so this was the route that took him back to Lord M, sadly sans tea.

Clog dancing in Shanghai

Mary Anne's dad did a bit of musing, and on reflection, decided that the thing to do was to go home – he was missing Mary-Anne's mum, Mary-Anne and Mary-Anne's lion, Ralph. So he packed his traditional muser's wheelie bag, found a nearby café – full of noise and the sound of clog dancing (Shanghai version – brought there by visiting East Anglian sailors) for some fortifying tea. Then off he went to the nearest tram stop. He had some trouble locating the one he wanted – most were going to various points in the city: the Bund, the Other Bund on the same side, the copy of the German capital, ß, Fish and Chip Town and so on – but he found it at last. It was stop 1 on the Belt and Road Initiative. 'Where you go?' said the friendly conductor, 'All the way,' said Mary-Anne's dad 'hun na hoo bo chi yuan prease.' Which language was that? In Mandarin it would be the equivalent of £4,600 give or take the odd halfpenny. In Cantonese it would be £13.60 exactly, which of course would be very reasonable.

'Would you like branket? Very co'd in Almaty.' said the kindly conductor. 'Is flee. Can rend. Return at Athen.' A certain British noble lord was already on the bus. 'Oh, hello, Frank.' said the newcomer 'Hello, your lordship,' said the other. Finally the tram got started and whined away.

Mistakes and errors

Eventually Lord M and Snidge were reunited and much were the expressionless faces, twitches of lips and barely discernible nods of the head which greeted their coming together. 'Where's my bloody tea, Snidge!' Lord M barked politely. 'I haven't quite found you any tea, My Lord,' bowed Snidge, 'but I have discovered a category error which I thought might interest you.' '"Error"! don'cha mean "mistake"?' 'Either may be used I believe sir, unless you are a particular kind of Logical Positivist, where the actual term is of paramount importance and it is not necessary to say anything about the error or mistake itself.' 'Can't get on with these Viennese jonnies myself, Snidge, coffee drinkers the lot of them.' 'I am inclined to agree your worship but there is in fact, if the silent rumour I have heard is the case, an actual mistake or error, quite near here.

Anaximander

'I wonder how your dad is getting on'/said Pontius, feeling the time had come/ to ask about the man he'd never met/ but they relied so much upon for tea. 'Yes, when did you last hear, Mum?' said Mary-Anne. 'tree mons ago, about, I sink.' said she. She got out her knitting and looked in the side pocket of her stool for the pattern. It was a complex almost three-dimensional portrait of Anaximander in the style of Praxiteles with highlights that looked forward to Hockney. In the absence of wool, which she had no notion of having yet been invented she used a spare bit of sacking.

Wittgensteinian Fideism

'Now where is it, exactly?' said Jenny, using all her powers of perspicacity, well all that were needed at that particular time, (not so many since she was standing in No. 17's shadow). 'Here it is. I wonder if they remembered to put in that extra button?' she said to herself in a thoughtful kind of way. Opening her Tractatus at random as was her wont, she hit upon the phrase 'two objects of the same logical form are – apart from their external properties – only differentiated from one another in that they are different (para 231)' which immediately inspired her to begin the assembly of arguments in favour of and contra the existence of the extra button, in the hope of arriving at an a priori synthetic answer to the vexed question., '… or I could have a look I suppose.' which is what she did.

Ducks' legs

'What does that lion do all day just being gentle.' said one of two ducks who were in idle conversation, 'Don't be silly, you can't do being gentle, gentle's something you are.' 'That's the problem Ralph has. He is caught fast in a linguistic nightmare.' 'I don't think it is a linguistic problem at all. I think it's a problem of non-linguistic reality.' And so they argued into the gloaming with only tea and cakes and later on game pie and beer to sustain them (they carefully avoided the duck's legs on offer and checked the local definition of 'game' before they started on the pie, which was lovely by the way). Meanwhile Ralph was getting a bit fed up.

Kyrgyzstan

The tram continued on its way, speeding up when going uphill and slowing down as its little nose pointed down (it was training to be a rocket in its spare time). It meandered (trams don't usually meander – it depends on where the tramlines go) downhill and up dale and eventually through a gap designed for the purpose through the Chinese wall into Kyrgyzstan where it stopped for tea. Ha-re-ram-den was the name on the clay wall of the tea shop and the befuddled passengers got down to share with the locals the strong tea flavoured with fermented yaks' milk which you had with welks, brought in by pantechnicon over the border from Tajikistan and hence subject to welk tax.

Breakfast

Snidge was speaking of course, of Ralph, currently busy practising being gentle and not being at all cross. He, Ralph, had no notion of category errors, or mistakes, whereas Lord M had spent his entire adult life occasionally allowing the concept to float for a brief moment into his consciousness, so he was a bit of an expert, well compared with some. 'Wotcha think of Ryle's *Concept* thing, Snidge?' (There had been an article on Ryle on the packet of seaweed flavoured muesli Lord M was in the habit of having for breakfast, for his first course anyway). Snidge had also allowed Ryle's idea to percolate into his thinking from time to time but had sometimes grappled with it to greater effect. He had reached page nine of the famous book, to where Professor Stackpole is eyeing his breakfast egg. 'I'm about to find out.' said he.

Entanglement

The third button was indeed present and this meant that Jenny could start thinking about her idea: the circuitry must be there for space and time travel (this was a standard feature) and it just needed to be hooked into the button, probably via a tiny bus-bar. The button would obviously need to have switchable verification/ falsification functionality and be entanglement capable, and there would need to be signalling of direct indicative statements in that large red lamp in its protective cage just over there. It could also be connected to a tea making facility so the traveller could whistle across aeons and light years and have a cup of tea ready upon arrival at her destination. All she needed now were a few partial differential equations and she thought there should be some lying about in that drawer there, among the spoons and forks, nicely wrapped in soft leather. 'That looks like a useful one,' she said, 'or perhaps that one, it's bit bigger.'

Field language game

In fact Ralph felt like being a bit cross. Spotting a passing lamb he said 'Little lamb I am a little bit extremely cross with you, er, sorry.' 'Wot's vat? 'oo are you to say fings like dat? Oi. You lot d'yhere wot this big tub o' lard just said to me? Wot's your game you great puddin'?' 'Oh er I thought you were someone else.' 'Well I ain't. Go an do your bein' cross wiv dem.' 'I'm very sorry if I've offended you, nice little lamb. I think it could be another linguistic mistake. I think I might have got into the wrong language game. I was expecting to find a field language game.' 'I don't know about any language games. We make up our own games 'ere.' and off he bounded.

'All in order'

There were quite a few bits of sacking lying around, from Mary-Anne's mum's various trades and occupations. One of the things she was hoping her husband would do when he got back was to get them all in order, which he was good at. She hoped that if nothing else, he would get back from China with a thorough working knowledge of Confucius, who was so good at order – 'hang nee pond li' no fum pee lit' was one of her favourite sayings which she had picked up from a leader in *The Illiterate Common Peoples' Literary Review* which Ralph had read out to her in Cow. 'I'm hoping that there is a quantity/ of tea. It would be in that pot just there.' said Pontius a little bit awkwardly. 'Yes,' said Mary-Anne's mum, omitting to pour any and turning to speak to her daughter.

In omni omnibus

Now Ralph was feeling increasingly peculiar as you might feel if you were the victim of a category mistake. He thought he'd consult his *De Rerum Natura* and see what it had to say about the matter. So he did so and checked the relevant section (The Nature of Mind and Spirit of course) and this gave him heart. As usual he sat there reading it with great concentration, especially the passage 'memmiadae nostro, quem tu, dea, tempore in omni omnibus ornatum voluisti excelle re rebus' and didn't notice the approach of Bets-y. 'What's the matter with you then.' said the cow. 'Oh moo,' said Ralph, 'am I pleased to see you!'

FISTTM

'Actually I'm not sure I need any buttons.' said Jenny to herself. 'If I remember correctly, I've set up these machines with (rather a primitive version of) voice recognition software.' 'Alexandra, where can I get some tea?' she said. 'I beg your pardon, I was snoozing.' said the machine. 'What did you say?' 'I said,' she said just a little too forcefully, 'where can I get some tea?' 'No need to shout. Find it yourself you little madam.' Jenny had never been called a little madam before and was slightly offended. She was a no-nonsense, down to earth FISTTM (Fellow of the Royal Institute of Space-Time Travel and Tea-Making Appliance Designers and Manufacturers) which was so important that it didn't have much time for madams of any size.

Guiding light

Mary-Anne's dad sat and continued to muse as he sipped his tea, adding and subtracting the milk until he got it just right and levering out some of the welks before tossing the delicious food thoughtfully into his closed mouth ('damn!'). Then he got out his Confucius and began to read. 'Won't do yer much good 'ere.' said a visiting Turkmenistanian seated at a nearby barrel, 'you need the little book of our great leader.' Mary-Anne's dad peered at him carefully (yak's milk always made him temporarily short-sighted and he was reluctant to put down his Confucius, now become his guiding light) before saying, in a very deliberate way 'Where would you get one of them?' 'You're in luck mate,' said his neighbour, 'I happen to be a great leader's little book salesman. I can let you have one for a hundred som.' At this point, Featherstonehaugh's brother, who had been sitting on the other side of Mary-Anne's dad's tree stump looked up briefly from his tank manual and said 'Perhaps I might have a look when you've finished?'

Polyglot

Ralph, unusually for a lion, was a polyglot and multi-linguist which is why he could speak Cow. To be fair Cow isn't difficult to learn as it consists of a single word, albeit with a rich vocabulary of connotations and moods. So he and Bets-y were able to sit down and have a wide ranging discussion on areas of mutual interest such as the correct use of categories, minor infractions and serious errors, and ice cream controversies. 'How nice it is sitting here in the sun having such a pleasant conversation.' He could see Bets-y becoming his new best friend. 'What on earth's that? Looks like a young woman on a tuppence halfpenny. But it can't be!'

An unfortunate woman

It was and it wasn't. Jenny had already reached No.17 but of course because it was a species of Space-Time machine, albeit with a lazy voice activated human/machine interface and it was, the machine, scanning around itself in space and time and had captured Jenny cycling across a field towards itself although in fact she had already arrived. The unfortunate woman was thus visible to Ralph although she wasn't there anymore – hence his cry of 'it can't be.' Ralph needed his solid and dependable new friend Bets-y to help him extract himself from this conundrum. If there's one thing category errors, if he was one, don't like, it's conundra.

Promptings of conscience

'Where *is* this bloody error Snidge?' 'It's in this lane here I'm sure.' said the redoubtable philosopher-menial, 'I'm sure I heard it talking to some lambs.' 'Well get on with it, it'll be getting dark soon and we won't find our way back, or to be precise, *you* won't.' 'I think I would, sir,' said Snidge, 'I'd follow the promptings of my conscience.' 'Would you by all that's justifiable.' growled the great lord, wondering the while where his steed had got to. Just then an enormous cat leapt out of the bushes – it was of course Ralph. 'Sorry, just practising being fierce, didn't mean to frighten you.' he said morosely and yet evenly, as if inspired by some great system of thought, or a rumbling tummy.

Pontiac

'What did you say votre ami's nom was, dear.' said Mary-Anne's mum. 'I can't quite remember.' said Mary-Anne, 'I only met him today, putting those notices up, then that thumping great mustachio'd clod on that donkey made us take them all down again.' 'Ze noticiees, 'ow wer zey about?' 'Names of trees, it's the only thing I care about, apart from the pre-Socratics.' and a tear began to form in her eye. 'You did say "let them name themselves" you know/does that bespeak the kind of love you claim?' said Pontius, eyeing the teapot. Mary-Anne now burst into tears. 'Classic Freudian defence,' she snivelled, 'and I remember now, your name's Pontiac or something like that. Let me pour you a cup of tea.'

Mystical

The tram continued its way over the wastes and deserts of the old Spice route, through the shifting sand, past caravans of camels and Moorish temples, nice little country pubs such as 'The Crown and Metaphysical Puzzlement' with their neat gardens overlooking the canal and oak timbered eateries, the cliffs with their inset golden buddhas, by the flimsy yet sturdy bridge over the thundering river and on ever westward, while Mary-Anne's dad pored over the great leader's little book (this one was green rather than the preferred red but had a slight mark on the cover in consequence of which a discount of two som had been agreed). He pondered the great leader's thoughts 'I am jolly important', 'no-one is as important as me', 'no-one except me is important', trying to glean the hidden meaning of the poetic and gnomic aphorisms that filled the book with their marvellous, stately and mystical language which glowed like visible perfume. 'Here we are,' he said to himself 'I am really, really important'. 'The repetition of 'really' suggests an underlying lack of confidence, could he mean 'inportant', ie not very portent?' he wondered? 'Could this be the key to everything there is?' It was getting cold. Mary-Anne's dad pulled the blanket up and nodded off as the old walled cities and oases slid past as in a dream.

'A tricky one indeed'

Ralph of course had no notion of time or space even if he was a philosophical puzzlement or category mistake, so could not make a distinction between Jenny arriving on her tuppence halfpenny and her having arrived on it, a tricky one indeed, and one that Jenny did not have to concern herself with, even if Ralph was left feeling tired and emotional by it all (it is well known that if you are a puzzlement or error, you are very prone to emotional tiredness and other ailments, such as crabapple foot; you may be of course, as Ralph was, a superb linguist). He continued his nice chat in Cow with the delicate and rather good-looking Bets-y as the latter chewed on some juicy and tasty bits of grass.

2413

So Jenny had another go: 'Machine No.17, please take me to Asteroid 2413 in Super-Argus and land me there, gently mind.' 'Alright, hop on.' 'I am on.' 'Oh yes. Would you mind trying to be a bit heavier?' The thing you have to watch out for with Asteroids is, if you are too rough with them they'll toss you off, that's why you will sometimes hear them called 'bucking asteroids' or 'bucksteroids'. The reason Jenny wanted to land on an asteroid is that dealing with something that likes to buck and either staying on while it does so or persuading it not too was fun. This was about the only fun thing she ever did. Otherwise she was more or less always serious and, if we're honest, a little bit sombre. That 'sombre' of course supplied an ideal hat for a spot of bucking, if you were Mexican that is, which Jenny wasn't, although she did know where Mexico was, well more or less, over the pond somewhere south of Trump. The more serious side of what she was looking for on 2413 was the wealth of materials it contained and their potential for mining – iron, zirconium, heterodoxium and so on of course – but also as yet undiscovered emoticons such as those applicable to the emotions appropriate to being in two places at once (texts sent by Schrodinger's cat might incorporate some of these).

In which Mary-Anne snaps

Pontius and Mary-Anne took their leave, well, there wasn't any cake or tea left so it was time to go. They went back up hovel lane to Main Lane. 'Did I just see a lion mooing to/ a cow?' said Pontius looking rather puzzled. 'I told you before it was a philosophical puzzlement.' said Mary-Anne, not without a little bit of crossness. Then her face softened, 'Well he's only a *boy.*' she mused and gave him a quick smile. 'I don't remember that,' said Pontius/'you said something about an error.' 'Same thing.' snapped Mary-Anne, 'Well, we'd better get to work.' 'What is there to do that must be done'/ said he, 'Commoners may not be idle.' 'You are in the right of it for once.' said she, 'That red-faced clodhopper will only complain if he finds us not toiling.' But what to toil at?

Dogmatic Slumber (2)

'There, Gracious Lord, is the mistake, or error.' confidently pronounced Snidge. 'Not much of one, I'd rather have a cup of tea.' replied his lordship, echoing Plato quoting Socrates on Hemlock. 'Find Aristotle and we'll go home, *if* you can find the way.' (he doubted whether Snidge could justify himself). Just then they came across the commoners they'd seen before. 'Where d'ya think you're goin' the great lord barked. 'Sorry, Your Worship, we didn't recognise you without your donkey.' 'Donkey!' bellowed Lord M, 'Yes, without your donkey and other accoutrements you look more like a poet or philosopher aus Wurtemburg.' said Mary-Anne, cleverly making use of her progress on Duolingo (it would have been even greater had she had access to a computer, if they'd been invented of course). At the mention of the sage of Wurtemburg and the simile conjured by the quite attractive youngish girl, the great Lord softened, 'H'mmph, well then, let me not see you further without the evidence of toil upon your hands, brow and rags.' said he reasonably. 'If I can intervene, your Majesty/ I toil in poetry, those fields/ of loveliness, whose bright reapings/ do justify the heavy toil of sowing.'

In which the conductor speaks with urgency

'Has anyone seen the crang,' said the conductor with some urgency, 'it seems to have disappeared.' 'Unress we find it, we cannot go on. It is against Imperirar, that is, sorry, Company legurations.' Mary-Anne's dad woke with a start, 'Bother.' he said. 'But I can see the point. It's unsafe not to clang, how else do tribesmen, aurochs, rickshaws, camels, spotted dogs and primitive combine harvesters know you're there? A device for clanging is essential safety equipment.' 'Mary-Anne's dad commiserated with the stricken conductor and asked if there was anything he could do. 'Find crang prease.' was all the conductor could manage to say before he entered a deep, but thankfully temporary, swoon. Mary-Anne's dad, using the experience he'd gained on the railway, organised the passengers into search parties and urged them on to action using exhortations from the little green book 'I embody importance', '*important* is the very least of what I am', sure that his intervention would soon produce the necessary result. Featherstonehaugh's brother tried to pull rank on him but unfortunately his level of understanding was not of the most elevated kind and he was forced to, or as he put it, 'insisted on' delegating the work to Mary-Anne's dad. He kept for himself the far more important job of reconnoitring the immediate area in case there was a tank museum.

Plethorae

Ralph and Bets-y were getting on like a barn conversion on fire. Their talk covered a plethora of topics from life in the countryside, how to feed humans, how not to frighten them, the impact of solitude, the nature of friendship, existentialism in small, cultivated fields, to the cultivation of bananas and other similar topics. 'Ralph, can I ask you a question?' said Bets-y, 'Moo.' said Ralph in a very encouraging tone of voice. 'Can you speak any other languages?' 'Moo' said Ralph in a way which bespoke much positivity. 'Which ones?' said Bets-y, 'Moo.' said Ralph in a Russian sort of way.

The Belt and Road Initiative

Next thing Jenny and No.17 found themselves in a baking hot desert very near some tram lines, and was that a stopped tram? 'What on earth have you done you ragamuffin,' expostulated she. 'Where are we?' said sleepy No.17. 'Not on a bucksteroid.' said the irate Jenny. 'Bucksteroid?' said No.17, 'I thought you said tram stop 2413 on the Belt and Road tramway.' 'Well, since we're here, said the disgusted inventor, I'd better go and see what's what.' So Jenny walked over to the softly humming tram. 'Hallo,' said Jenny, 'have you stopped to pick up passengers or is there a problem.' 'Our crang's bloke.' said the newly awakened conductor. No linguist, Jenny replied 'Eh?' at which point a westerner appeared, speaking in Turkmenistani 'The importance of our great leader cannot be overstated' said he. 'Eh?' said Jenny, who was by no means a philosopher. 'Oh sorry, what Li Peng (Mary-Anne's dad was now on first and second name terms with the conductor, although he hadn't yet been able to work out which was which) needs is an inventor.' 'I'm your girl' said Jenny brightly, 'what seems to be the problem.' 'Our clanger's gone astray.' said the dad, 'That's not a problem, I can invent one. Is there a foundry near here?' 'There's one over there, by the ruined tank museum.' 'Oh yes, I can see it, behind that thorn tree. And what's that creature doing there tied to it?'

In which Lord M loses his voice

Lord M was rendered speechless by the shining jewel of peerless poetry issuing from the mouth of a commoner, and a badly dressed one at that. 'Gad,' he said when he had recovered himself. 'were you about to cut that tree down?' he said pointedly, 'don't let me stop you, but I'd like to converse with you some more, providing you don't get too close.' And he transferred the equivalent of a few coins from the account on his phone, to that of Pontius, conveniently lying at his, Pontius's, feet. 'I have no thought of killing trees,/ but if you wish to have some tea ... .' 'Tea.' said his Highness, 'I hadn't thought of that. Take me where is tea.' 'There's a tea shoppe just down the lane.' interjected Mary-Anne, not wishing the boy Pontius to get all the attention. 'I, that is we, will take you there. Where did you put your mule?' 'Snidge, find Aristotle and follow us, if you please.' and off they trooped.

In which they do not go up to Oxford

Mary-Anne's mum sighed and interrupted her reverie on the subject of the absence of her husband. 'I'd bettair va and lait ze cows.' she muttered to herself. 'Ou sont-ils? In ze lane I suppose.' So down (or was it up? No, one only goes *up* to *Oxford*) the lane she went and was surprised as she approached her favourite field to overhear an interesting conversation 'Can you moo discursively, my friend Ralph?' 'Moo.' replied he in a French intellectual (Merleau-Ponty or the earlier Althusser come to mind) kind of way. Mary-Anne's mum was a little surprised but realised she had little time for that kind of emotion with the Olde Milke Boarde breathing down her neck. 'There are two creatures there, I wish I could remember which one is good for milk. I know, it's the one that says 'moo' and she led the docile Ralph to the milking parlour. This was an extension of the tea shoppe and provided all the milk for the many cups it supplied every day. Mary-Anne's mum hoped that Ralph was pasteurised. Luckily he was. 'Oh, 'ang on a minute.' she said, 'Sacred blue!'

Diagram

Long into the afternoon Snidge searched for his lord's steed. Finally he came across a thorn tree. 'Well,' he said to himself, 'I've found a tree, there seems to be horse here, but also a desert and a foundry, not to mention what looks remarkably like a down at heel tank museum, and what's that, a tram?' Seeing before him a girl in bicycle riding gear, peering down alternately at a slim volume and up at the foundry, Snidge thought he'd better speak to her, out of politeness if nothing else, oh, there was something else – extreme puzzlement. 'Excuse me miss, I am reluctant to interfere as I see you are hard at work, but, if I may, just for a moment, I am wondering why the English country lane with a tea shoppe where I thought I was has changed itself into a desert with a tram and a foundry not to mention what looks like a tank museum, although it might be defunct.' Jenny looked up from her Tractatus, sliding a lemon into it so as not to lose her place (lemons in this part of the world tend to be as slim as Tractati, though not as enthralling, even if they do taste better – flat lemons are less tart of course). 'Oh, that'll be a philosophical puzzlement.' said she and showed him the diagram on page 37.

'Quoi now'

Mary-Anne's mum quickly led Ralph out of the parlour and left him in the van park with a couple of vegan black puddings. 'Moo,' he said in a meek, excursive kind of way. 'C'est suffit, avec les "moo's".' said Mary-Anne's mum, with some vigour 'zat were not 'elpful aujourd'hui.' 'Roar.' replied Ralph, like one who wishes to shout but can only whisper. 'Quoi now?' said Mary-Anne's mum as the visitors began to arrive: His Majesty Lord M, Pontius Pilates and Maid Mary-Anne come for their tea, which they could hardly be expected to drink without milk. 'Here is the tea-shoppe that I promised you/said Pontius, a smile upon his face.' Despite himself, but backing away slightly, the great lord could not restrain a little and rather genuine-looking smile as he signalled which table the commoners should sit at, quite close really to the one he'd chosen for himself, in the absence of Snidge, who would normally be expected to carry out such lowly tasks, in between rehearsing the arguments for the existence of God proposed by St Anselm or trying decide whether Langer's distinction between 'discursive' and 'presentational' forms was valid (Ralph clearly thought it was, but he could be a bit of a simpleton in these matters and in any case he was in the van park).

'You may call me Jenny'

'That's fixed it.' said Jenny with rare satisfaction as she gave the new bell a soft tap. 'Well done!' said Mary-Anne's dad, 'Ms. er … ' 'Renne, but you may call me Jenny.' 'How do you do, I'm Frank.' 'I thought you were.' 'What now?' 'Where are you going? Can I give you a lift?' 'Can *we*?' It turned out that Jenny and Frank both wanted to return to the green and pleasant land where they had discovered they were neighbours, if not immediate ones. Should they go by tram, rather slow but reliable, or by Space Time Logic Chopping Machine (STLCM), potentially very fast but wayward. They debated this for a time during which the tram, now rather late, clanged its bell and went on its way. 'That's a nuisance, I didn't give the blanket back,' said Mary-Anne's dad exhibiting a profound sense of shame, 'on the other hand, I left it on the tram. But I am sad not to say goodbye to Li Peng.' For his part Li or Peng was sad not to have had the opportunity to say farewell to Frank, but 'time and tlam wait for no-one.' As it passed, Featherstonehaugh's brother gave them all a regal wave from his tram window. He was off to Lop or possibly Lop Nor (or even and somewhat improbably Tashkent) where he would change tram for Novokuznetsk which had not only a small but well managed tank museum but also boasted the finest selection of Siberian tea in the local area. Snidge, who had been waiting politely while these exchanges took place and the tram had left now said a little shyly 'may I join you on your trip?'

In which they sit at table

'We'd all like tea s'il vous plait.' said Mary-Anne's mum, taking contrôle. 'Yes dearie.' said the proprietor, a small person with an apron upon which she was wiping her hands, a person straight out of Rousseau, Emilia her name was. 'Lemon, fresh in from Kyrgyzstan?' 'No, milk.' 'We haven't any milk. Lime? Honey? Crumbled chili-flavoured biscuits?' 'No milk?' 'No. We had a lion in here and it frightened all the milk away.' 'Maintenant what?' muttered Mary-Anne's mum loudly but inaudibly (depending which side of the table you were sitting at).

No.17 is hungry

'Home, No.17.' said Jenny pointedly to the sleepy machine, 'What? Where did you say? I'm hungry, give me some logic to chop.' 'I haven't any, but there is some at home.' 'Oh that's your game is it?' 'I'm not playing games, I just want you to take us home.' 'I know where your home is, but where are theirs'?' 'Take us to my home!' said Jenny, now exasperated, 'and now!' 'Terms like "now" are meaningless to me.' 'Here *and* now!' 'That's more like it.' and off they went. 'I'd better take that container of yak's milk for the journey,' said Mary-Anne's dad, 'even if it is fermented.'

The validity of inferences

And so it was that yak's milk saved the day in the tea shoppe. For imagine the embarrassment for the young people and Mary-Anne's mum. They, the young people, had brought the great man to the tea shoppe with an implied promise of tea, from which promise one is normally entitled to infer the presence of milk. Indeed there are only two essential items for tea shoppi (this is the ancient plural of shoppe, also used in some parts of Italy) to pass the eponymous test – tea and milk (for the pernickety, there is a third item, the bath bun, but this need not concern us here). The lines 'Shame is the thing I feel at this juncture/ I never shall hold up my head again.' came to Pontius's lips. 'Me neither.' said Mary-Anne, 'Et, what of moi. I am responsable for ze lait.' grogné Mary-Anne's mum as the full horror of the situation dawned on them all. But at this very point, who should burst through the window of the tea-shoppe (they hadn't had time to find the door) but Jenny, Snidge and Mary-Anne's dad. And not long after that,

Featherstone's brother appeared, although he, of course being a conventional kind of person, actually came through the door. In the ensuing delight of the re-acquaintanceships, which it would be invidious to dwell upon, Mary-Anne's mum could not help but mutter 'vous ne have pas of milk I suppose.' 'Yes, as a matter of fact I do.' and so they all continued relaxed and happy (even the upper lip of Lord M might have been observed almost to be on the point of quivering) with their rather rich tea. 'Ahem,' said the brother, 'as an alternative, you may wish to try my Siberian tea, which is normally imbibed black.'

'Blushing a little'

This put them all in a really good mood. Eventually his highness signalled to Snidge to lower his tea-pouring posture so that he could whisper into his ear, 'Ahem,' said Snidge rising his full servant height (he was of course somewhat shorter than his lord, perhaps something to do with his diet of dripping and stones), 'Male commoner no.1, his lordship requests that you regale him and indeed all of us with a further sample of your speech.' Blushing a little Pontius took a breath, 'Honour it is to me and all my fam/ ily to speak before our highness lord/ and ... .' 'What's the blighter saying, Snidge? What's that about muses? That kind of talk usually means money.' 'Yes, sir, it may do so, though I doubt it in this case. I have formed the opinion that this young person simply enjoys his gift and wishes to share it with others.' 'H'mm, you may be right but we can't take any chances; any ideas Snidge?' 'I have one my lord: one might set up a poetry workshop to include him and the others at The Manor or at a room in this tea-shoppe should they have one available. No-one would expect payment for an appearance at a workshop, unless he were the chair, which in this case of course, you would be as the senior in poetry as well as being of higher social rank. It would cost you no more than a pot of tea, with proper milk of course, perhaps a biscuit or two, and a cake at Christmas. And we might be able to be economical with the cake, sir. I could have a word with the young woman's mother who I understand makes a very high quality medieval marmalade gateau which she might be willing to trade for some of my dripping and stone cake which you kindly let me make for Christmas.'

Pantoums, haibuns and farewell

So it was that the great Manor Poetry Workshop came about, Lord M chairing. Anyone in the area who showed the slightest poetic ability and some who did not (although for some reason lions, cows, lambs, ducks and foreigners were not invited whatever their abilities, perhaps because Maid Mary-Anne had abruptly insisted upon from thenceforward being styled Person Mary-Anne and farmyard animals, category mistakes and Turkmenistanians could not be relied upon to recognise nice distinctions) would be seated round the great table with notebook and pen or in some cases propelled pencils (propelled by Snidge in the case of Lord M); Snidge fussing over iambics, dactyls, pantoums, haibuns and the like and supplying the necessary exercises, waste paper derived writing paper, photos, trigger words, etc and obtaining tea and biscuits at the behest of His Grace; Pontius and Person Mary-Anne sitting shyly together; Featherstonehaugh and his brother eagerly discussing the brother's discoveries and the details of Pushkin's stanzaic forms; Mary-Anne's mum and Jenny discussing the invention of poetry in France and of course Mary-Anne's dad, dreaming of that great work he was going to write, just as soon as he'd learnt how to push a pen. At least he could count on plentiful supplies of paper (No.17 had been left waiting grumpily outside, converting piles of wastepaper into writing paper, as if preparing for the composition of magni opi). The variety and range in quality of the poetry produced was great. The very best was gathered up by the indomitable Snidge and placed in a folder marked 'His Lordship's Poems'.

Bio

Robin Thomas has had six books of poetry published – *A Fury of Yellow* (Eyewear 2016), *Momentary Turmoil, A Distant Hum* and *Reminded of Something* (Cinnamon 2018, 2021 and 2023), *Cafferty's Truck* (Dempsey and Windle 2021) and *The Weather on the Moon* (Two Rivers 2022) – and a Novella in Flash – *Margot and the Strange Objects* (Adhoc 2022).

Printed in Great Britain
by Amazon